PERMISSION

EXPLICIT EROTICA

JUST PLAIN BOB

WARNING

This book contains sexually explicit scenes and adult language. It may be considered offensive to some readers. This book is for sale to adults ONLY.

Please store your files wisely where they cannot be accessed by underage readers.

* * * * * * * * * * * * * * * * * * *

About the Publisher

4Fun Publishing, a member of **BLVNP Incorporated**, 340 S. Lemon #6200, Walnut CA 91789, info@blvnp.com / legal@blvnp.com
NOTE: Due to the highly emotional reaction of some people to works of erotic fiction, any email sent to the above address that contains foul language or religious references is automatically deleted by our anti-spam software and will not be seen. All other communications are welcome.

DISCLAIMER

Please don't be stupid and kill yourself. This book is a work of FICTION. Do not try any new sexual practice that you find in this book. It is fiction and not to be confused with reality. Neither the author nor the publisher or its associates assume any responsibility for any loss, injury, death or legal consequences resulting from acting on the contents in this book. Every character in this book is over 18 years of age. The author's opinions are not to be construed as the opinions of the publisher. The material in this book is for entertainment purposes ONLY. Enjoy.

Permission
Explicit Erotica

By: Just Plain Bob

This is another "Be careful what you wish for" story. It is a story of how a lot of love can be as damaging as a little hate. It is a story about two people and how they managed to screw up their marriage.

* * *

Kathy and I had been married almost ten years. We met as the result of an accident. I accidentally backed into her car in a parking lot. The damage looked minor, but you can never can tell about things like that. There was no one around so I wrote a note and put it under her windshield wiper. She called me that evening about six and I suggested that we get together and exchange insurance information and all the rest of what she would need to file a claim.

She was a college student and had just gotten out of class and my office was only eight blocks from the campus so we settled on a seven o'clock meeting at Angie's, a student hang-out just off campus. I told her that she would recognize me immediately because it was almost certain that I would be the only one there in a three piece suit and tie. She laughed and said she would probably be the only one there with flaming red hair.

I spotted her right away when I got there. She was sitting in a booth and I walked over, introduced myself and sat down. I asked her if she had eaten yet and when she said that she hadn't, I waved the waitress over and ordered a large Angie's brick oven pizza.

"No anchovies work for you" I asked Kathy and she told the waitress, "No anchovies and extra pepperoni."

When the waitress was gone I pulled out my insurance card and driver's license and handed them to Kathy and she passed me a piece of paper that she had already written her information on. After she had copied my information she handed me back my stuff and said:

"You are an interesting man."

"In what way?"

"Most people would have just taken off and hoped that the damage wouldn't be noticed for days. In fact I probably wouldn't have noticed if not for your note,"

"What can I say? I just had a feeling that the car belonged to a gorgeous redhead with green eyes and I knew that the best way to meet her would be to hit her car and leave a note."

She looked at me for a second or two and then she smiled and said, "Damned if I don't almost believe you. And what were you going to do when you met this fantasy woman?"

"Get to know her better."

She was twenty-two, a senior, and working toward a degree in Marketing. She had interned at the same company two summers in a row and she had been invited to apply for a full time position when she graduated. She was single and not in a relationship at the time.

From me she learned that I was three years out of school, working for an investment firm downtown, single and just out of a relationship that had turned bad. Then I asked her:

"How many am I going to have to kill to be first in line outside your door?"

"I don't know. Tell me more about this relationship that went bad. Whose fault? Hers or yours?"

"Hers mostly, but maybe a tiny bit mine."

"Do I get an explanation of that?"

"I caught her in bed with another man so I would say that the fault was mostly hers, but I have to accept the fact that I might have done something to put her there."

"Like what?"

"I've no idea, but there had to be a reason she went from me to him."

"Did you ask her why?"

"No. What would be the point? She made a choice and once that choice was made we were done. No need to talk about it."

"I'll have to say it again; you are definitely an interesting man. Most men that I know would have laid it all at the feet of the woman who cheated. Not one of them would have said that maybe some of it was their fault."

"Back to my question about the line in front of your door."

"You have my number. If you call maybe you can take cuts."

I did call and that led to a one year courtship that ended with Kathy being my bride.

* * *

Kathy was a virgin when we married, but she took to sex like a baby duck takes to water. She wanted to try it all and of course I obliged her. We quickly found that light BDSM and water sports were not for us, but Kathy did love to be eaten, loved sex in any position we could make work, had massive orgasms when we had anal sex and she would willingly swallow whatever her blow jobs could produce.

As the years went by things started to slow down a little in the sexual department. It wasn't so much a lack of desire as it was a case of same old/same old. Kathy had a higher sex drive than I did and she wasn't going to let things go stale. She began to look for ways to take the staleness out of things. Some of the things she came up with bothered me a little, but I felt that it was my lot in life to keep the woman I loved happy so I usually went along with whatever she came up with.

She thought it would be a kick to make love on the back seat of the car out at the local lover's lane at Steven's Point. We did it and I'll admit it was exciting, but I also sweated getting caught by the cops. Kathy got such a charge out of it that she wanted to do it again and over the course of the next year the back seat, and the front seat, saw plenty of action at Steven's Point, the Safeway supermarket parking lot, the Wal-Mart parking lot, two rest areas on the Interstate and various side streets in town.

One night we were sitting on the couch watching television when Kathy stood up, turned off the set and said:

"I want to go for a walk."

We walked outside into the bright full moonlit night and I asked her which way she wanted to go and she said down to the park. We walked down to the park which was eight blocks away and when we got there Kathy tried the swings for a bit, talked me into getting on the teeter-totter with her for a while and then she went over to the monkey bars. She played around for a bit and then she hiked up her skirt, pulled off her panties and told me to take out my cock. I looked around and didn't see anybody so I complied. Kathy got up on the monkey bars and arranged her body and then said:

"Get over here and fuck me lover."

Imagine if you can, Kathy with her feet on one set of bars, holding on to a higher set of bars and pushing out so her body looked like a sideways "u" that put her sexy ass at just the right height and position so that all I had to do was step forward and slide right in. Add to that it was a bright, moonlit night and anyone coming into the park couldn't possibly miss seeing us. It was wild! Over the next six months we tried the swings, the teeter-totter, several picnic tables and of course – we spent a lot of time on the monkey bars.

Then there was Kathy's prostitution phase. It didn't do much for me, but it turned Kathy into a sex fiend which in turn rocked my world. What Kathy did to me when she got wound up was dynamite.

It happened by accident. Kathy's car was in the shop and I was working late so I couldn't pick her up when she got off work. As a senior accounts manager Kathy was usually the last one to leave the office. She usually got off around five-thirty to five forty-five. She was going to come to my office and when I finished up we would go home from there. It was a little after six and just starting to get dark and Kathy was standing on the corner of Fourth and Sherman trying to make up her mind as to whether she should flag down a cab or take the bus when a late model Caddy slowed to a stop next to the curb. The passenger side window slid down and a voice said:

"How you doing Sweet pea?"

Kathy bent down and looked in the window and said, "Pardon me?"

"I asked you how you were doing honey, but we both know that what I'm asking is how much?"

As soon as he said that Kathy knew what was going on. The man thought she was a hooker standing on a corner. At first she was pissed. Granted, she was wearing a short skirt and heels, but the skirt wasn't all that short – it was just above the knee – but she didn't think she looked anywhere like the street walkers she had seen while driving around town and she was all set to dump on the guy when she changed her mind. Why call him a pig when she could string him along and then leave him hanging.

"How do I know that you aren't a cop?"

"Oh come on honey; you know cops can't solicit. That's entrapment."

"Cops have been known to lie to make an arrest stick."

"We both know that in this town to make a prostitution arrest valid they have to have it on tape."

"Tapes can be edited."

"Okay, how about this. You don't say nothing, just shake your head yes or no. You are a classy looking lady so what do you say to a hundred and I pay for the motel room?"

Kathy shook her head no and made an upward motion with her hand.

"One fifty?"

Again Kathy shook her head no and made an upward gesture with her hand.

"Two hundred?"

She shook her head no again and unbuttoned her blouse and showed him her 34Cs encased in a frilly bra. She leaned forward and gave him a good look at her cleavage and cupped her tits with hers hands. He took a long look and then said:

"Three hundred?"

Kathy smiled and reached for the door handle. She saw the guy's eyes light up and she pulled her hand back from the door handle.

"Show me."

"Show you what?"

"You know. Do the one thing that a cop would never do. Show me."

"Oh, I get it" he said and he unzipped and pulled out his cock. He stroked it a couple of times and Kathy watched as it came erect.

"Satisfied now?"

She grinned and reached for the door handle. She had the door opened about six inches before she pushed it shut and said:

"Sorry, but something about this just doesn't feel right."

She spun on her heel and walked away smiling as he screamed, "You fucking bitch!"

When he pulled away she flagged down a cab. When she got to my building she came into my office, locked the door behind her and then asked me if I had a twenty dollar bill. I said I did and she asked me to give it to her. I gave it to her and she said:

"I could have gotten three hundred for this, but I'm giving you the family discount so you only have to fork over twenty."

She lifted her skirt, took off her panties and then turned and bent over my desk.

"Hurry baby, hurry. Fuck me like a twenty dollar whore"

She was wet when I slid into her and all I really had to do was stand there while she went nuts driving back at me. When it was over I asked her what got into her.

"It wasn't what got into me lover; it is what wanted to get into me" and then she told me the story. "You want to know the weird part? I really wanted to get into that car and find out what it would be like to fuck some stranger for money."

That was the start of it. From then on, at least once every two weeks she would go out and walk on the street until someone pulled over and tried to pick her up. I was always parked where I could watch her and be close enough to get to her if there was trouble, but there never was. She always pulled that, "Show me. Do what a cop would never do and show me" and then after the guy had pulled out his cock she would say something didn't feel right and walk away. When she'd had her fun we went home and she fucked me into near exhaustion.

* * *

The next thing that came along was the result of an accident. Kathy had gotten into a fender bender and her car was in the body shop being repaired. Until she got it back I was dropping her off at work in the morning and picking her up at night. She got off work a half hour before I did and one night instead of sitting in the lobby of her building and waiting for me she called me and told me she would be waiting for me at the lounge just down the street.

When I got to the lounge I found that it was happy hour and the place was packed. Kathy was sitting at the bar with a Rob Roy in front of her and three guys talking to her. It took me a minute or so to push through the crowd and I came up behind her just as the guy on her left said:

"It is only ten minutes from here and I really would like a woman's opinion on how to decorate it."

"I'd really like to" Kathy replied, "but I can't tonight. Maybe some other time."

"I'm here every night for happy hour."

"I'll remember that."

"Are you sure .." and at that point I tapped Kathy on the shoulder and she turned and said:

"Oh, there you are."

She picked up her purse and got up. As we walked toward the door Kathy said:

"I have to use the little girl's room before we leave."

"I need to go too. I'll meet you out front."

"Make sure you wipe it down good lover; it is going to be in my mouth as soon as we get in the car."

I was sitting in a stall when someone came in and I heard a guy say:

"I ought to kick your ass for butting in on me like that. I would have had her if it wasn't for you."

"Bullshit! She was waiting for that guy."

I recognized the voice of the second guy as being the voice of the guy who had been trying to get Kathy to go to his apartment. I could hear the sound of their whizzing as the first guy said:

"It didn't matter. She was ready. I saw it in her eyes and if you hadn't butted in I'd have had her out of here before the guy she was waiting for got here. She wanted it dude; it was as plain as day that she wanted it."

I heard the second guy over the sounds of the sink as they washed their hands:

"If she really wants it she'll be back. I told her I was usually here every night for happy hour."

"Maybe so, but I don't know about another night. What I do know is that she was a sure thing for tonight."

"Water under the bridge my man. Let's see what we can do with those tw…" and the door closed behind them. I washed my hands, met Kathy outside and we went and got in my car. She slid over next to me and her hand went to my zipper.

"Hurry home lover" she said as she worked my cock out. "I'm horny as hell and I need to be laid."

As she was stroking my cock she said, "Did you see them trying to pick me up? They wanted me. They really wanted me. They were trying to get me out of there before you could get there."

She lowered her head and took me in her mouth and as she worked to bring me off I thought about what I had seen when I first got to the bar. I thought about it and I knew what was going to be coming up next. What had happened turned Kathy on and Kathy would do just what she had done when exhibitionist sex turned her on and just what she did when the prostitution thing turned her on. She would want to do more of it until something newer came along.

Kathy was riding me cowgirl and talking about her time at the bar.

"They wanted me lover; I know they wanted me."

"I know they did" I said and I told her about what I'd overheard in the men's room.

"They could see that? They could tell from my eyes that I wanted them? They knew from my eyes that I was ready? I was lover, I was ready. It's weird baby, but as he talked I really did reach the point where I wanted to go to his apartment. It was the same feeling I had when the guy in the Caddy tried to buy me. I wanted to get in that car. The very same feeling lover, I really wanted to go to that apartment."

"Would you have gone if I had not have shown up?"

"Of course not! Fuck me lover, fuck me hard. Get me off lover; make me cum."

* * *

It was two days later when I came home to an empty house. That was odd since Kathy always beat me home. Maybe half an hour after I got home Kathy came in. She dropped her purse on the table, gave me a passionate kiss and said:

"Bedroom. Now!"

She pushed away from me and headed for the bedroom dropping clothes along the way. I knew my lines in the play so I followed her undressing as I went. In the bedroom she pushed me back on the bed and then she mounted me. As she rode me cowgirl she said:

"I stopped by the lounge after work. He wasn't there, but I hadn't been on the bar stool long enough to get the cushion warm before I had a half a dozen guys trying to hustle me. They all wanted me."

She was pounding down hard on me and moaning. "And I wanted them baby, I wanted them. Fuck me baby, fuck me hard."

I pulled her down to me and rolled putting her on her back and then I drove hard into her. Hard and fast while she cried out:

"Make me cum baby, make me cum."

She had an orgasm and she dug her nails into my back and ass and moaned:

"More baby, more."

I was able to give her one more before I reached my climax. As soon as I was out of her she spun around and went for my cock with her mouth and went to work at getting me back up. It was an exhausting evening. When I couldn't answer the call any more we lay there and I asked:

"Do you think it is wise for you to go into that bar alone?"

"What's the matter baby, don't think I can handle myself? You don't trust me?"

What could I say to that? I gave her a reassuring pat on the arm and got up to go to the kitchen to fix us a bite to eat.

The next day was a repeat. She got home a half hour after I did and pulled me straight into the bedroom.

"He was there tonight" she said as she rode me. "He wants me. He wants me bad. We talked about his apartment and me looking at it to give him a woman's perspective. He wanted me baby, and I wanted him. I wanted to go to his apartment in the worst way. Oh God baby, fuck me."

It was two days before it happened again. Same story. "He wants me" she moaned as she bounced up and down on my cock. When we were done she said:

"He keeps trying to get me to go to his apartment." She hesitated for a moment and then said, "I told him tomorrow. I told him I would meet him for a drink and then we could go and look at his apartment."

"You what!" I almost screamed as I pushed her away from me.

"Don't go getting all wound up on me baby. I'll meet him, have the drink and when we get up to leave the bar you will walk in and say something like, 'Oh there you are. I was hoping to find you here.'"

"One of these days Kathy your little games are going to backfire on you,"

"There you go again; not trusting me to be able to handle myself."

Wisely I kept my mouth shut.

The next day Kathy called me at work and gave me her game plan. She would walk into the lounge at a quarter to six. She would order her drink and nurse it until six and then she would order another. At six fifteen she would tell the guy she was ready to go. That would give me plenty of time to get to the lounge and get into position to intercept them as they were leaving.

It was as if I had been looking into a crystal ball the previous evening when I told Kathy that someday one of her games was going to backfire on her. I hadn't gotten a block from work when I ran into a traffic jam. An accident was causing traffic to back up for blocks. Finally the two vehicles were pushed out of the way and traffic began moving again. When I pulled into the lounge parking lot it was twenty to seven – a good twenty-five minutes later than Kathy's six-fifteen!

I went inside not having a clue as to what I was going to find. Had Kathy gone to his apartment when I hadn't showed? The first thing I saw when my eyes adjusted to the light level was apartment guy sitting at the bar talking with a couple of other guys. I looked around and didn't see Kathy. As I was looking around the place a waitress came up to me and said:

"You look like a Rob; am I right?"

""Yes, I am a Rob."

"Kathy said to tell you to go back out to your car and wait" and then she walked away.

I took one more quick glance around and then went back out to the car. I sat there maybe two minutes before I saw Kathy come out of the place, look around, see me and head for the car.

"Where were you" she asked as she got into the car. I told her what had happened and then asked her what had happened.

"We were almost at the door and you weren't anywhere around so I told him that I had to make a quick trip to the ladies room before we left. And then I described you to one of the waitresses and told her to tell you to wait in the car for me."

"You hid out in the bathroom for almost half an hour?"

"The alternative was I would come out and go with Hal to his apartment. Would you rather I have done that?"

By then I was just a little pissed by her attitude. The "would you rather" and all the recent "What's the matter, don't you trust me" she had thrown at me had me a little wound and I snapped:

"Why not? It is what you wanted to do anyway."

Kathy gave me a nasty look and we proceeded home in silence. There was no mad, passionate love making in our house that night.

* * *

That night put an end to Katy's stopping at the lounge and in a couple of days things were back to normal between Kathy and me. Kathy waited a week and then she hit me with her next idea.

"I had fun going to that lounge and teasing guys. I want to do it again, but at some different places only I don't want to risk any more traffic jams. We can go to a place and you go inside and get a seat where you can watch what goes on and then I'll come in and take a seat and we will see what happens. Or I'll go in first and then you come in."

I knew better than to say, "No thanks, I don't think so." Besides, I didn't see where things could go wrong with me being there as Kathy's safety valve. Silly me, right?

The first couple of dozen times there were no problems. Kathy would take a seat at the bar or at a table and then the guys would try to move in on her. She never had to pay for a drink (other than giving out a dance or two) and after she had a sufficient number of tongues hanging out she would get up and leave and we would go home and fuck like sex crazed bunnies. Did either one of us think that what she was doing was terribly bad? Hell no! She had her wedding rings on and the guys still came after her any way. They deserved the blue balls they went home with.

But Kathy likes to push the envelope. She began dressing sexier. Low cut blouses that showed plenty of cleavage. Short skirts that showed plenty of leg. Sexy high heeled 'come fuck me' pumps. When the guys asked her to dance she let them get closer. She allowed their hands a liberty or two. I sat and watched and got more and more uneasy about things.

Then on our twenty-sixth time things got out of hand. It started out like a usual night. I went in first and picked out a spot where I could see most of the place. Ten minutes later Kathy came in and took a seat at the bar. Within minutes she had a guy move in and offer to buy her a drink. More guys, more drinks and then she was out on the dance floor. Guys pulled her in close and grinded against her. A hand went to her tit and she pushed it away. Hands went to her ass and pulled her in tight and she didn't push them away.

I was sitting there and getting more and more pissed at what was going on and I was on the edge of my seat on the verge of going out on the dance floor and dragging Kathy out of the place when the band took a break. Kathy got her purse and headed for the ladies room and a second or so later the guy she had been dancing with, the one who had put both of his hands on her ass, got up and followed her. I still to this day don't know what made me do it, but I got up and followed along.

At the end of the hallway that led to the bathrooms there was a storeroom and I got to the hallway just in time to see the guy trying to pull Kathy into that storeroom. I hollered "Hey!" and ran down the hall toward them. Stupid move on my part. The "Hey!" gave the guy enough warning that he was able to set himself up to meet me. By the time the bouncers pulled us apart the guy was missing three teeth and I had a broken nose. Kathy was blubbering and trying to stop my nose from bleeding with a handkerchief and I pushed her hand away and snarled:

"Leave me the fuck alone!"

The ride to the hospital was silent and after my nose was set in the ER the ride home was just as silent. We were in the house before Kathy said:

"Why did you holler at me to leave you alone?"

"Because you were the one who caused it. You just had to let those assholes put their hands on you more and more and you never stopped them and that led up to me having to fight some asshole who was going to rape your teasing ass. You couldn't just let things be. You just had to dress sexier and sexier and go farther and farther to feed your goddamned 'excitement' jones and I get to be the guy who pays the price."

"You also got to be the guy who got all the benefit from it or did you forget that part?"

"Yeah, but is it worth the price I have to pay sitting there watching and seething as you let asshole after asshole take liberties with you? I don't think so. No more Kathy, no more!" and I stomped off to bed.

Things were a little chilly around the house for about a week and then on a Saturday I woke up to Kathy sucking on my cock. When I was fully awake Kathy said:

"I'm sorry baby, please forgive me, I'm sorry."

* * *

Six months went by without Kathy coming up with any more ideas. Our sex life settled down some to two or three times a week. It was nice easy love making, but there wasn't any of the wild passion that had been there when Kathy played her games.

One night after we had made love Kathy asked me if I had any fantasies of a sexual nature and I told her that I didn't have any. Then I asked her why she had asked.

"I don't know; just curious I guess."

"Do you have any?"

She looked away for several seconds and then said, "One."

"What is it?"

"I'd rather not say."

"If I had said yes when you asked me that question and then tried to duck telling you what it was you would have badgered me until I told you so I'm not letting you get away with stonewalling me. What is it?"

"You couldn't handle it."

"How do you know I can't handle it?"

"I know you Rob. I know that there isn't any way you could handle it."

I wouldn't give up and I kept after her until she finally relented and told me. My jaw hit the floor when she said:

"I want to make love to another man while you watch."

I just stared at her for several seconds and she said, "Well?"

I finally found my voice and said, "Well what?"

"What do you think?"

"I don't know what to say. That was totally unexpected."

"Well at least you didn't sputter and yell out "Hell no."

"What? You expected me to say, 'Sounds like a good idea?'"

"A girl can hope."

"You are so dissatisfied with me that you want another man?"

"Don't be silly Rob. I am absolutely satisfied with you."

"Then what the hell is with this other man shit?"

"It isn't shit honey. You know I was a virgin when we got married and you know how quickly I took to sex. I've always wondered what I missed by staying pure until I walked down the aisle. I've always wondered what another man would be like. Remember me telling you how badly I wanted to climb into that car when the guy thought I was a hooker? And the time I told you that I really, really wanted to go to that guy's apartment? It isn't a new fantasy sweetheart; I've had it for years and years."

She leaned over and kissed my cheek. "I'm not at all interested in replacing you baby. You will never have to sweat that." She turned and shut off the light and cuddled up next to me and in minutes she was asleep. I was on my back staring up at the ceiling as visions of Kathy climbing into strange men's cars and going into strange men's apartments moved through my mind. It was very unsettling.

The next morning over breakfast I asked, "Could you really make love to another man?"

"It is just a fantasy Rob, not reality."

"I'm curious. Why do you want me watching?"

"So you will feel a part of it. I couldn't do it alone because that would seem too much like cheating. If you were there it would be like you were putting your stamp of approval on it."

"You would expect me to approve of you fucking other men?"

"Not 'other' men honey, just one. Just to see what it would be like."

"It doesn't sound like you are talking fantasy now. It sounds like you really want to do it."

She looked away from me and didn't say anything so I let the subject drop. But not talking about it and not thinking about it are two very different breeds of cat. I could not get it out of my mind that Kathy wanted to fuck another man. Kathy said that she'd had the fantasy for years and years and I wondered why she had suddenly brought it up. I wasn't stupid. I knew Kathy and I knew that she knew me well enough to know that if she asked me about my fantasies that I would ask her what hers were. And she knew that when she hedged I would stay on it until I got it out of her. The question was why did she want me to know? Why now after all these years? The answer that I came up with – rightly or wrongly – was that she was on the edge of doing it and she wanted me to say it was okay.

Well it wasn't okay!

I didn't want my wife fucking another man. It wasn't my fault that she was a virgin when we got married. That was her choice. If she would have had fifty sexual partners before we got married it wouldn't have mattered at all. I would still have married her. God knows that I spread my share of pollen before we got married. What happened before the engagement and the wedding vows was none of my business or hers. No! No fucking way did I want her sampling another man.

But then I was left with the question of would she do it anyway even if I didn't say that it was okay. The answer that I came up with to that was unsettling to say the least. I did not think that she would deliberately set out to do it, but if the right set of circumstances occurred it could happen even if she hadn't been looking for it. I remembered how she was when we played her game at the bars; how she got progressively more accepting of what her dance partners were doing. If I hadn't been there would she have gotten worked up enough that without even thinking of what she was doing she would let something happen?

And another thing. Something that I hadn't thought of before. When I saw the guy pulling Kathy toward that storeroom I was keyed on him and not her. Was she trying to fight him off? Trying to pull away from him? Was she so into what they had been doing on the dance floor that she was going to let something happen? I had no answers to those questions. There were some answers though. If she did it behind my back and I found out would our marriage continue? No! If she told me she decided to do it and went ahead after I said no would we still have a marriage? Again the answer was no.

Should I ignore it and hope it would go away? How in the hell could I do that? I would always be waiting to hear the other shoe drop. After a week of rolling it over and over in my mind I came to the realization that it was going to happen. Sooner or later Kathy was going to do it. If she did it and I never found out we would be okay. But I would find out. I knew Kathy well enough to know that she couldn't hold it in. She wouldn't be able to live with the guilt. Sooner or later she would confess and then we would be toast.

I loved her and I didn't want to live my life without her in it, but if she cheated on me, she was gone. The only way I could see making our marriage last was to allow her to have her fantasy. And it was going to happen. I knew it was almost a certainty. A girl's night out, stopping for drinks after work with the girls she worked with, a party where she had quite a bit to drink, any one of those combined with the right set of circumstances and it would happen. I had to give her my permission because if it happened without it we were through.

I sat on it for a week and thought and re-thought it and finally I bit the bullet. Over dinner one night I flat out asked Kathy:

"Is your fantasy really just a fantasy or do you really want to do it?"

She looked at me for several seconds and then she said, "I want to do it."

"I want you to think long and hard on this Kathy. I don't know how I am going to handle it. Are you willing to risk your marriage just to satisfy a fantasy?"

"It won't hurt us Rob. I'll just be satisfying a curiosity. I won't be looking for any emotional involvement."

"That's what you say now, but what happens if your lover gives you a bigger or better orgasm than I do. What if he is more sexually satisfying? What if you try another man and it is so different for you that you want to try a third and then a fourth to see how much different they can be?"

"I wouldn't do that. Only the one Rob, I swear – only the one."

"I wish to God you had never brought up the subject. I don't want it, but you have put me between a rock and a hard place. Damned if I do and damned if I don't. If I say yes and don't handle it well our marriage might not survive. If I say no and you do it anyway our marriage would be over."

"I would never do it without you knowing."

"You say that now and you could very well mean it, but time changes things. You say that you have had this fantasy for years and years and for those years and years the fantasy kept getting stronger and stronger until it was so strong that you brought it out in the open to see how I would respond. The only reason for doing that is because you have reached the point where you really want to do it. You want my blessing, but the big thing is that you want to do it and you will still want to do it even if I say no fucking way. So three, six or nine months from now something happens that would give you your chance to try it without me ever knowing. How strong would your fantasy have grown by then? Strong enough that you might take the chance?

"Think back to the guy who thought you were a hooker; you really wanted to get in that car with him. Or the guy who wanted you to go to his apartment. You really, really wanted to go do it with him. What if something similar happens a year from now? With your fantasy getting stronger and stronger as the months go by would you back away or would you get into the car or go to the apartment? That's what you have me looking at now Kathy. Say yes and it doesn't go right and we are done. Say no have you do it anyway and we are done. The only thing I can do is say yes and hope to God I can handle it or hope that you will realize what a huge gamble you would be taking and decide that it wouldn't be worth what you would lose. Take your time Kathy and really think it through and then let me know what you want to do."

"I don't need to take any time Rob. I want to do it and I know that everything will be fine between us. I love you and you know I do and you love me and I know it. There is nothing that can tear us apart. I'm glad you are nervous over it. If you would have said, "Oh sure Kathy; go ahead and have a good time" I would have been hurt that you could care so little about it. I know how unsure you are about it because I've had all the same thoughts myself, but I'm positive that everything will be okay between us.

The fact that you will trust me to do it just makes the bond between us all that much stronger."

"All right then Kathy, go ahead, but one thing. I'll be in the house somewhere, but I will not watch. That would be just too humiliating for me."

"But you have to be there Rob. I can't do it if you aren't there."

"Then I guess you aren't going to do it."

"Please Rob. That's the only way I can do it and really know that it is okay with you."

"No Kathy. No way! I'm not going to stand there while another man uses you and smirks at me while thinking, "Can't take care of your wife? Watch how a real man does it."

"Please Rob. Do it for me, please?"

"No Kathy. I'll be in the house – in the next room even – but I will not watch and at no time will I let whomever you pick see me or will I see him. Listening will be bad enough and that is as far as I'm willing to go."

She was silent for several seconds and then she asked, "When can I do it?"

"That's up to you Kathy. I'll let it happen, but I won't have anything else to do with it."

"I think I'd like to do it next Friday. I'm not insensitive to the way you feel and I think we will need to do some serious hand holding after it is over. If we do it Friday that will give us the weekend alone."

"Next Friday? Isn't that kind of quick? Or do you already have someone picked out?"

"No I don't, but I need to get this out of the way before you back out on me. I'm a fairly good looking girl. If I can't come up with someone within an hour of my walking into whatever place I go to it will be a serious blow to my ego." She leaned over and kissed me. "Thank you lover. Thank you for loving me enough to trust me on this and thank you for being mine."

* * *

The week passed by quickly and all too soon it was Friday. Work sucked all day. I couldn't get what Kathy would be doing that night out of my mind and I couldn't blame anyone but myself for my mood. I was the one who said yes. I thought back to the night when Kathy said:

"Thank you for loving me enough to trust me."

The reason I agreed to go along with it was that I didn't trust her. I didn't trust that someday her fantasy and circumstances would come into perfect alignment and she would get carried away and do it. That she would feel guilty after I didn't doubt, but it still would have been cheating, and when I found out, our marriage would be over.

So there I was. Sitting at my desk at work and trying to wrap my mind around the fact that I'd told my wife she could have sex with another man in the hopes of keeping her and saving my marriage. How weird was that?

I was a nervous mess when I got home from work. I tried to find projects around the house that would maybe keep me busy and keep my mind off of what was going to happen later. The plan was that Kathy would get off work, hit a bar or lounge, pick up a suitable sex partner and then call me when she was on the way home. Kathy got off work around five-thirty and the call came at five after six. That sure didn't take long I thought. Her ego sure wouldn't be suffering any.

It was a hot August day and I was working in the basement. Because of the heat I had the windows open and I was standing by the one that faced the front yard and was just to the left of the front porch. I heard a car door slam and two people talking as they came up the walk. The voices became clearer as they got closer and as they were walking up the front steps I heard:

"Are you sure that he isn't in there waiting for me with a baseball bat?"

"Don't worry about it. I told you; he is all right with this."

"I have to admit that when you told me two months ago you could get him to go for this I thought you were nuts. I hope you were worth the wait."

"Oh I am sweetie. I can promise you that you won't be disappointed."

I stood there stunned.

She told him two months ago she could get me to do it? Two months ago? And then something else registered. I knew that voice. I couldn't picture who it was, but I'd heard that voice. I wiped my hands on a rag and headed upstairs. Kathy and her stud were already in the bedroom and undressing when I walked in the bedroom door and I saw why the voice was familiar. It was apartment guy. Kathy saw me and smiled thinking I'd changed my mind and was going to watch. The smile disappeared when I said:

"Pull your pants back up sport. You might get to fuck the bitch, but it ain't going to be tonight and it ain't going to be here. Maybe in that apartment you were so eager to get her to. Right now you need to saddle up and move out before I get that baseball bat you were worried about."

"Rob? What are you doing? You said th…"

"Shut up Kathy."

"You said it wa..."

"I said shut up Kathy. One more word out of you and I'll push you out the door right behind him and you can follow him to that apartment that you really, really wanted to go to."

She wisely shut up and stayed silent while I watched 'apartment guy' hurriedly dress and then head for the door. Once he was gone I told Kathy that she could sleep in the bedroom since she had fouled it with 'apartment guy's' presence and I would sleep in the spare bedroom.

"Tomorrow when I'm calmer we can talk and decide where we go from here, but you might as well know now that things don't look too good and you might want to start making a list of what you want to take out of the wreckage of our marriage.'

And then I walked out of the room before she could say a word, went out and got in my car and headed for the nearest bar. It was after midnight when I got home and Kathy was waiting for me in what used to be our bedroom.

"Rob honey, we need to tal..."

"I don't need a fucking thing from you Kathy except your fucking silence. I said we would talk tomorrow."

I grabbed my pillow off the bed and went across the hall to the spare bedroom. I locked the door behind me and it wasn't more than a minute before Kathy tried the door knob. Finding the door locked she knocked and called out:

"Rob? We need to talk Rob. We need to talk now Rob, not tomorrow, but now."

I put my shoes back on, opened the door and pushed by her. I got in my car and drove to a motel. In the morning I had breakfast at an IHOP and then around ten I went home. I found a red-eyed and haggard looking Kathy waiting for me when I got there.

"Where have you been? I've been worried sick."

"You wouldn't leave me alone like I told you so I left and went to a motel."

"But why did you behave like that last night? You told me I could go and then you went all freaky on me. I don't understand."

"You should. You have had all night to think about it."

"Think about what? You told me I could do it and then you went nuts on me."

"Think back to what I said to your stud. The part about going and getting the baseball bat he was concerned about. When did he mention me being inside waiting for him with a baseball bat?"

"When we were on the porch. But I told him that he didn't have to worry because you were okay with what we were going to do."

"What else did he say?"

"I don't know Rob. We were both a little nervous and we talked, but I don't remember about what. We were talking to hide our nervousness from each other."

"Well let me tell you what I heard. I believe the exact words were, "I have to admit when you told me two months ago you could get him to go for this I thought you were nuts." Remember it now? You have been planning to fuck that asshole for over two months now. Playing me for a fool. Or have you already been fucking him, but just wanted the extra thrill of doing it in front of me? I can't believe I fell for it. I listened to your "I just want to try another man once just to see what it would be like." Leading me to believe that it didn't matter who, just as long as it was someone different. Yeah, right! Didn't matter who and all the time the two of you were setting me up."

"It wasn't that way Rob."

"Oh no? Then what was with that bullshit you fed me Thursday night. 'If I can't find someone within an hour of walking into whatever bar I go to it will be a serious blow to my ego.'" You told me that already knowing where you were going and who you were going to bring home. You played me for a sucker Kathy. You played me and I fell for it. All I can say is that I hope that it was worth it. As far as I'm concerned all that's left is to divide our stuff and call the lawyers."

"You can't be serious Rob."

"Of course I am. I need to get away from you Kathy. I don't want to be around when you start spreading pollen. I'll get out of the way and you and apartment guy can get on with what you were planning on doing."

I shook my head in disgust and muttered, "Two months. Two fucking months. I can't believe that I was so stu…"

"That's enough Rob!"

"What?"

"I said that is enough!"

"That isn't nearly enou…"

"Shut the fuck up Rob! If you think I am going to sit here and listen to a one sided rant you are crazy. You wouldn't talk to me last night, but you are going to listen to me right now. I have never had sex with Hal. I have never had sex with anyone but you. Did I want to have sex with Hal? Yes I did. With Hal or with someone else. Or Rob, or! Did I set you up as you claim? No I did not. I involved you, not set you up. My fantasy of wanting to experience another man has been getting stronger over the years, but as bad as I wanted to do it there was no way – no way Rob – that it was ever going to happen without you being on board with it. I don't care how strong the urge it is not going to happen behind your back.

The first step was to let you know what my urges were and see how you would respond. I asked you about your fantasies knowing that you would ask me about mine and that is just how it happened. I explained to you what I wanted to do and why and you said I could. That brings us to Hal. Two days after the traffic jam aborted our plan for Hal I went back to the bar to talk to him. I stop in there every once in a while with some of the people from work and I wanted to be able to stop without having a problem with him. I told him that I was sorry, but there was no way we could do anything because of my feelings for you. I told him that when I came out of the bathroom I saw you and so I ducked back in and waited until he got tired of waiting for me and either left or went back to his seat at the bar."

"Every time I did stop he was there and he kept trying and I kept saying no, that I couldn't cheat on you and one day when I said I couldn't cheat on you, that there was no way I would go behind your back he said:

'Then don't go behind his back. Ask him if it is okay.'

I told him that he was out of his mind and he said that he had heard of men who let their wives play around and that I'd never know if I didn't ask. That gave me the idea of bringing you into my fantasy. I asked him if he could perform while being watched and he said that it wouldn't be a problem. So yes Rob, I did line him up as my partner two months ago and there was a reason for it. Did you think I was silly enough to walk into a bar, pick up some stranger and bring him home and take a chance on picking up a disease and passing it on to you? I told Hal he could be the one if I could talk you into it but he would have to bring me a letter from his doctor stating that he was disease free. That takes a little time. He got the letter for me two days before you gave me the go ahead."

"Was I trying to be sneaky? Not one bit. I knew you would recognize Hal as soon as you saw him and don't give me any of that crap that you would never see him. You might not stay in the room and watch, but I know you Rob and there was no way – no fucking way – that you weren't going to take a quick peek and see who it was."

"What about the charade of going out Friday and all that shit about your ego?"

"Would you have let me go if I had said, 'Okay, I'll go pick up Hal and be right back?' I was gambling that once we were here you would accept it as a done deal and let it happen."

"Even if what you say is true I still feel like I've been tricked. When I asked you if you had someone already picked out you lied to me and said you didn't. You played me Kathy and I'm not the least bit happy about it. You know how reluctant I was to let you do it to begin with so you should have made damned sure that everything you did was out in the open and completely above board. You should have told me about Hal. Would I have been happy about it? Probably not, but I wasn't happy about the whole thing anyway. Would I have understood why if you had explained it beforehand like you did just now? Yes I would have and I probably would have accepted it as a sign of clearheaded thinking, but the way you did it smacks of dishonesty.

"You said it yourself. You were afraid that I wouldn't let you do it if you told me you were leaving to go get Hal. That means that you knew what you were doing was wrong. I told you up front that if I said yes and it didn't go right we could be done and even knowing that you tried to hide things. And after all the years we have been together you don't know me well enough to know what I would think when I saw you with Hal? Given your sexual nature and all the games you like to play didn't you know that my first thought was going to be, 'I wonder how long this has been going on?' You didn't think I wouldn't wonder how many times you had been to that apartment that you really, really wanted to see?"

"That's not fair Rob. I have never cheated on you."

"I only have your word for that Kathy and right now, with the seeds of doubt and mistrust you have planted in my mind your word isn't worth all that much."

"You can't seriously believe that I would have done that."

"Right now I don't know what to believe Kathy. It has been over six months since the night I was supposed to stop you from going to his apartment. That means that you have been seeing him and talking to him for six months and since you have always been home on time that means that you had to have left work early to meet with him. How early did you leave work? Early enough to go over to his apartment? You have opened a can of worms Kathy and they all crawled out and wiggled away. You are going to play hell trying to get them all back in the can."

"You aren't making sense Rob. Think about it. If I was already doing Hal why would I need to bring him here? Why wouldn't I just keep my mouth shut? And besides, if you heard the thing about the baseball bat and the two months then you also heard him ask if it was going to be worth the wait. Okay, I went about it the wrong way, but I wanted it and you had said yes and it was just so close to happening that I didn't want anything to stop it once it got started.

"I'll say it again Rob; I have never been unfaithful to you and I would never do anything that you were not aware of."

There were several very long moments of silence and then Kathy said:

"What now?"

"I don't know Kathy. I have a lot on my mind right now and a lot to think about. For the time being and as long as you leave me alone I'm going to be staying in the spare bedroom. If you keep bothering me like you did last night I'll move out and do my thinking somewhere else."

"That's not fair Rob. You are treating me like I've cheated on you and I haven't."

"You haven't been honest and aboveboard with me either, Kathy and that is just as bad."

I got up, went up to our bedroom and started moving my things over to the other bedroom while Kathy sat in the living room and cried.

* * *

And that is where things are now. I've been two weeks in the spare bedroom and Kathy and I are stepping gingerly around each other. I still don't know what I'm going to do.

~~The End~~

My other BEST SELLING books available on Amazon!!

The Playmate: Erotic Romance

Frankie just can't keep his pants on long enough as not one, not two, but four women are hot on his tails.

Allison is the next-door neighbor, who has been in love with Frankie since childhood. Their mothers are already planning their wedding. But when Frankie comes back from Guard training, Allison is already dating another guy.

So Frankie hooks up with Allison's rival, Gloria. They are great in bed. However, Gloria goes to college several states away and she, too, can't keep her pants on long enough.

Frankie moves on to gorgeous Sarah. But staying faithful is so much harder than Frankie originally thought especially after he meets Vangie, Sarah's mother.

Just as he is having a hard time juggling two women, Allison and Gloria come back to his life.

What's a young man to do?

The Risk: Taboo Erotic Romance

Rob goes steady with one of the hottest girls in high school, Mickey. But he learns that Mickey has not been faithful to him so he gets it on with her best friend Bev. But lust and love keep pulling the two of them together, so they get engaged.

Mickey goes off to college while Rob stays behind to work. Eventually, their sensual weekends get less and less. And Rob hears that Mickey is going steady with a football player. So Rob makes mind-blowing bed scenes with an older woman, Alicia. But as always, Mickey wants him back.

There's no looking back for Rob, though, even when Alicia breaks it off with him. Why stick with a cheater when the pool of women is drowning him?

Will Rob be successful in evading Mickey? Or will true love and the steamy chemistry prevail?

Restless Spirits: Hardcore Gay Shifter Story

By: Angus MacGregor

You can run from anyone, but never from yourself.

Eli Bungo has looked for a family to belong to his whole life. Growing up as an Ojibwa native in Michigan on the shores of Lake Superior is a lonely and isolated existence. He longs to fit in but something inside tells him he doesn't. *And more than that—he has a spirit within that he doesn't understand. With only his beloved grandfather to guide him, Eli slowly comes to terms with the darkness within himself: a secret both terrible and amazing.*

As he moves from boyhood to adolescence, Eli is confronted with his true nature.

Learning Together

By: Dick Parker

Taylor has had a hard time of it for a few years. The twenty-four year old gets in with the wrong crowd and wastes his life through drugs and a general lack of direction in life. When he finally hits rock bottom – on the disgusting floors of jail, he decides to turn his life around, enrolling in a vocational program to become a plumber.

He lands a job with the handsome and older, Derrick, who owns a plumbing company and the two eventually become friends easily - too easy. When Derrick gets jobs in a neighboring town that only require two men, he asks Taylor, of all people to work with him. The jobs end up making them stay over in a motel for the week.

As the week passes by and as they become better friends, Derrick hints his interest in Taylor's past and present sexual escapades but reveals that he's married but when Taylor finds out that Derrick's wife is a manipulative woman who tricked him into marrying her, in the one room they're both staying in suddenly, everything becomes all too close.

With Derrick teaching young Taylor all about plumbing, can Taylor end up teaching this old man new tricks, about sex?

What Happens at Night: Taboo Short Stories

By: Amy Redek

What do you dream about?

Enter the world of dreams, where hidden intimate desires creep on you from the depths of your imagination, pleasure you, and wake you up thirsty for more.
A dream! It was a damn nightmare.

But it's not always a fun ride. Your mind plays tricks on you and blindsides you with elements you least expect—the kind of suspense that only builds you up.

Follow these 13 dreams of different surreal, fantasy, and sexual scenes, and discover a part of your own dreamland where your own hidden desires lurk—where only you know and enjoy.

The Laura and Shontay Chronicles: Hot Lesbian Erotica

By: Miranda Mars

"Should I see how wet it is with my finger . . . or my tongue?"

Laura has never been shy with her many trysts night after night, different women after another with one thing in common: hot and gorgeous black women just the way she likes it.

Pleasing too many women can be a little exhausting, but when her eyes land for the first time on the mysterious beauty that is Shontay, and seeing her around work, Laura's growing attraction for her can't make her stay away.

When she later runs into this new woman at her apartment, Laura finds the perfect opportunity to break through the seemingly cold-mannered Shontay. Soon the two women start an affair so intense they can't get enough of each other but Laura's wayward relationships with other women makes their relationship get a little complicated. Somehow, and without fail, they always keep coming back to each other for more and each time hotter and more intense than the last.

Check out the list of all my books!

The Prodigal Family: The Abbotts

Watching My Shared Wife

The Waitress and the Runaway Husband

Baiting Mr. Little

Too Hot for Henry

Chuck's Fantasy

The Redhead's Desires

Rescued at Riley's

His Every Fantasy

Open Mike Night

Pursuit for Revenge

Why Does He Do That?

Halloween & Drugs

Tracey

When Rob Met Kari

Becoming a Shared Wife, Vol. 1 –

(Wife Sharing and Other Adventures)

Becoming a Shared Wife, Vol. 2 –

(Hazardous Wives)

Becoming a Shared Wife, Vol. 3 –

(Wives Who Stray)

Becoming a Shared Husband, Vol. 1 –

(Suck Me)

Becoming a Shared Husband, Vol. 2 –

(Husbands Who Stray)

Becoming a Shared Husband, Vol. 3 –

(Get even!)

Becoming a Shared Couple, Vol. 1 –

(Steamy Swingers)

Becoming a Shared Couple, Vol. 2 –

(The Share Thing)

Becoming a Shared Couple, Vol. 3 –

(Kathy is Wild)

Erotica Short Stories, Vol. 1 –

(Taboo Desires)

Erotica Short Stories, Vol. 2 –

(Nasty Steps)

Erotica Short Stories, Vol. 3 –

(Married But…)

Erotica Short Stories, Vol. 4 –

(Sizzling 10)

Erotica Short Stories, Vol. 5 –

(In My Wife's Panties)

Erotica Short Stories, Vol. 6 –

(Taboo Unlimited Desires)

Erotica Short Stories, Vol. 7 –

(XXX Stories)

WANT FREE COPIES OF MY BOOKS?

Just visit my blog and download free copies of my books:

awesomeauthors.org/justplainbob